First Facts™

Animal Behavior

Animals Finding Food

by Wendy Perkins

Capstone
press
Mankato, Minnesota

First Facts is published by Capstone Press,
151 Good Counsel Drive, P.O. Box 669, Mankato, Minnesota 56002.
www.capstonepress.com

Library of Congress Cataloging-in-Publication Data
Perkins, Wendy.
    Animals finding food / by Wendy Perkins.
    p. cm.—(First facts. Animal behavior)
    Summary: Simple text explains the varied ways in which such animals as spiders,
zebras, and the yellow tang fish find their food.
    Includes bibliographical references and index.
    ISBN 0-7368-2508-8 (hardcover)
    ISBN 0-7368-5160-7 (paperback)
    1. Animals—Food—Juvenile literature. [1. Animals—Food.] I. Title. II. Series.
QL756.5.P46 2004
591.5'3—dc22   2003012182

Editorial Credits
Erika L. Shores, editor; Jennifer Bergstrom, series designer; Wanda Winch, photo researcher;
    Eric Kudalis, product planning editor

Photo Credits
Bruce Coleman Inc./Karl and Kay Amman, 10–11; Wardene Weisser, 13
Corbis/Roger Tidman, 16–17
Corel, 5
Creatas, 9
Image Ideas Inc./David van Smeerdijk, cover
McDonald Wildlife Photography/Joe McDonald, 8, 20; Mary Ann McDonald, 6–7
Minden Pictures/Gerry Ellis, 14
Tom & Pat Leeson, 15, 19

**First Facts thanks Bernd Heinrich, Ph.D., Department of Biology, University
of Vermont in Burlington, Vermont, for reviewing this book.**

1 2 3 4 5 6 09 08 07 06 05 04

Table of Contents

Time to Eat 4

All Animals Need Food 7

Grazing for Food 8

Predators Attack 10

Waiting for Food 12

Using Tools 14

Scavenging for Food 17

Finding Food 18

Amazing But True! 20
Hands On: Eat Like a Chimpanzee 21
Glossary 22
Read More 23
Internet Sites 23
Index 24

Time to Eat

Winter is coming. A chipmunk quickly gathers acorns and nuts. The chipmunk must store food in its nest. The chipmunk eats the acorns and nuts during winter. When spring comes, the chipmunk must find more food. It will eat **insects** and berries.

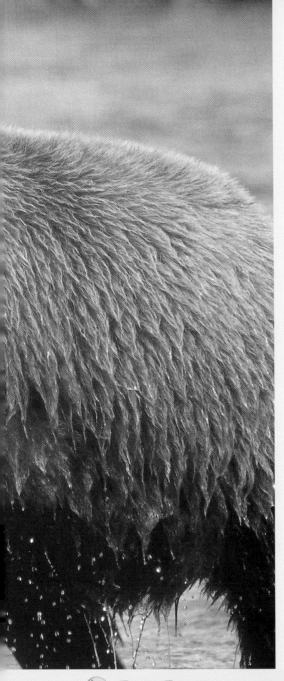

All Animals Need Food

All animals need food to live. Animals have different ways of getting food. Some animals hunt other animals for food. Some animals search for food. These animals eat the food right away or save it for later. Most animals spend much of their time finding food.

Fun Fact:
In summer and fall, bears can eat about 80 to 90 pounds (36 to 40 kilograms) of food each day.

Grazing for Food

Animals that **graze** move from place to place as they eat. Zebras look for a grassy area. They stop to eat. The zebras then move to another spot to graze.

A yellow tang grazes in tropical oceans. This colorful fish swims along a **coral reef**. The yellow tang eats **algae** growing on the coral reef.

Predators Attack

Some **predators** catch their food by surprise attack. Lions hide in the tall grass near a giraffe. The lions rush out of the grass. They chase and attack the giraffe. All of the lions share the meat.

Waiting for Food

Some predators wait for food to come near. A trapdoor spider waits in its **burrow**. The spider can feel an insect moving along the ground above. The spider jumps out. It drags the insect inside the burrow and eats it.

 Fun Fact:
A trapdoor spider makes a door for its burrow out of silk and soil.

13

Using Tools

Some animals use sticks and rocks to eat. A chimpanzee pokes a stick into a termite mound. Termites climb onto the stick. The chimpanzee licks the insects off the stick.

A sea otter bangs a clam against a rock. The clam shell breaks. The otter then eats the meat inside the shell.

Scavenging for Food

Scavengers eat dead animals. Vultures search for dead animals other predators leave behind. Vultures have sharp beaks. Their beaks cut into the skin of dead animals.

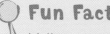 **Fun Fact:**
Vultures are the only birds with a good sense of smell.

Finding Food

All animals do what they must to find food. Chipmunks gather acorns and nuts. Zebras graze for food. Lions hunt for food. Trapdoor spiders wait for insects. How does an elephant find food to eat?

Amazing But True!

A person could swallow a watermelon in one gulp if people ate like snakes. Snakes can swallow animals larger than their own heads. A snake's jaw can open very wide. Some snakes swallow rats. Some of the world's largest snakes swallow goats.

Hands On: Eat Like a Chimpanzee

Chimpanzees use sticks as tools. A chimpanzee pokes a stick into a termite mound or ant nest. Ants or termites climb onto the stick. The chimpanzee then licks the insects off the stick. Try this activity to see how a chimpanzee eats.

What You Need

raisins
cup
pretzel sticks
peanut butter or cream cheese

What You Do

1. Put a handful of raisins in the cup.
2. Cover the bottom half of a pretzel stick with cream cheese or peanut butter.
3. Close your eyes. Chimpanzees cannot see into a termite mound. Put the pretzel stick into the cup of raisins.
4. Move the pretzel stick around a little bit. Then lift the stick out of the cup.
5. Open your eyes and lick the raisins off the pretzel stick just like a chimpanzee licks off insects.

Glossary

algae (AL-jee)—small plants without roots or stems that grow in water or on damp surfaces

burrow (BUR-oh)—a tunnel or hole in the ground made or used by an animal

coral reef (KOR-uhl REEF)—a strip of stony matter made up of the remains of small sea animals; a coral reef lies at or near the surface of water.

graze (GRAYZ)—to eat small amounts of grass or other plants

insect (IN-sekt)—a small animal with a hard outer shell and six legs; an insect's body has three parts.

predator (PRED-uh-tur)—an animal that hunts other animals for food

scavenger (SKAV-uhn-jer)—an animal that looks through waste for food

Read More

Richardson, Adele D. *Lions: Life in the Pride.* The Wild World of Animals. Mankato, Minn.: Bridgestone Books, 2002.

Schaefer, Lola M. *Zebras: Striped Grass Grazers.* The Wild World of Animals. Mankato, Minn.: Bridgestone Books, 2002.

Stonehouse, Bernard, and Esther Bertram. *How Animals Live.* New York: Scholastic, 2004.

Internet Sites

FactHound offers a safe, fun way to find Internet sites related to this book. All of the sites on FactHound have been researched by our staff.

Here's how:

1. Visit *www.facthound.com*
2. Type in this special code **0736825088** for age-appropriate sites. Or enter a search word related to this book for a more general search.
3. Click on the Fetch It button.

FactHound will fetch the best sites for you!

Index

acorns, 4, 18
algae, 9
attack, 10

beaks, 17
bears, 7
berries, 4

chase, 10
chimpanzee, 14
chipmunk, 4, 18
clam, 15
coral reef, 9

elephant, 18

giraffe, 10
grass, 8, 10
graze, 8, 18

hunt, 7, 18

insect, 4, 12, 14, 18

lions, 10, 18

meat, 10, 15

nuts, 4, 18

oceans, 9

predators, 10, 12, 17

rock, 14, 15

sea otter, 15
search, 7, 17
scavengers, 17
snakes, 20
stick, 14

termites, 14
trapdoor spider, 12, 18

vultures, 17

yellow tang, 9

zebras, 8, 18